A LION FOR THE KING

Retold by Meryl Doney
Illustrations by Cha Li

A LION PICTURE STORY
Oxford · Batavia · Sydney

This is a story of what might have been.

It begins long, long ago, when the beautiful land of China was ruled by the Emperors of the Han Dynasty. They lived in great palaces, surrounded by many servants. They wore clothes of silk and ate off plates of gold, and their people made many discoveries in science and art.

Learned men called astronomers studied the stars, making maps and charts of their movements.

Lao Zhou, the chief astronomer, and his assistant Jiang lived and worked at the great observatory on Green Jade Mountain . . .

Little Han was just twelve years old. His mother and father were both dead, so he lived at the observatory and worked for the chief astronomer and the assistant astronomer. He watered the flowers, tidied the scrolls and looked after the wonderful equipment the astronomers used.

In return, the assistant astronomer was teaching Little Han the secrets of the stars. Little Han hoped that one day he too would be a great astronomer. Maybe the greatest ever known.

One morning the chief astronomer called to him. "Little Han, Little Han, come quickly. Bring my scrolls and star maps. We must go and see assistant astronomer Jiang at once."

"Why? What has happened, Chief Astronomer?" asked Little Han in surprise.

"Last night, while I was watching the stars, I saw a strange sight. I want to know if Jiang saw it too," replied Lao Zhou.

"A strange sight? What kind of strange sight?" asked Little Han excitedly. But the chief astronomer took the star maps and hurried out. Little Han had to run to keep up with him.

When they arrived, Little Han's teacher was studying the great star charts.

"Have you seen them too, Jiang?" cried Lao Zhou.

"Indeed I have," replied Jiang. "And I have been awake all night, searching my charts for the meaning . . ."

Little Han could hardly contain his excitement. "What is it? What have you seen, Teacher?" he asked, jumping up and down.

"A new group of stars in the sky. There is nothing like them in all my charts," replied Jiang. "Come to the main tower tonight. We will look for them again."

That night the sky was clear. It sparkled with a million stars.

The astronomers prepared their instruments and trained the sight tube towards the north.

"There they are again!" cried Jiang. He made some careful measurements. "And more amazing. The stars have moved a degree to the west since last night."

The chief astronomer confirmed Jiang's calculations. "It is very strange," he agreed. "Such a beautiful bright group. It must mean something very important."

"Please may I see?" asked Little Han, who had been trying to wait patiently.

"Yes, Little Han," replied Jiang, letting him put his eye to the sight tube. Little Han felt a tingle run down his spine. There, in the middle of the circle of dark sky, shone the most beautiful star he had ever seen. And round it shone three others, like courtiers gathered round a king.

"This is the last and oldest of my charts," sighed Lao Zhou, "but there is no sign of these stars."

"Last night I found something in the writings of the ancient astronomers," replied Jiang. "They foretell the coming of the 'royal star'. Could this be the one?"

"We need wisdom beyond our own, Teacher Jiang," replied Lao Zhou. "We must go and see Lao Meng. She knows the writings of the ancient ones, of wonders on earth and signs in the stars. She will know what this means."

And so the two astronomers and Little Han set out for Lao Meng's home, high in the mountains.

"Welcome, Chief Astronomer Lao Zhou, Assistant Astronomer Jiang. And welcome, Little Han," said Lao Meng in her low, musical voice. "I have been expecting you."

Lao Meng made them sit down and served them with tea and rice cakes. Then she said, "I too have seen the 'royal star' of which you speak. I believe it tells of a great one who has been born thousands of miles away along the Silk Road to the west. He may be a king; he may be even greater. The stars are calling us to find him and to learn the truth for ourselves."

"Then we must follow them," replied the chief astronomer.

Little Han was so excited that he could hardly breathe. For three days he had been helping the astronomers prepare for the great journey. And Jiang had said that he could go with them. He, Little Han, might see the great king with his own eyes!

"The road will be dangerous," said Jiang seriously. "We must take only the most essential things. But we will need gifts for the rulers of the lands through which we must pass."

"And we will take gifts for the king," added Lao Zhou. "We will pack them in this plain wooden box, for there may be robbers on the way."

Little Han thought to himself, "What could I give to a king?" He had only one really precious possession, left to him by his mother and father. After a long moment he took from his room a small package, carefully wrapped in cloth, and slipped it into the plain wooden box.

"**G**oodbye! Goodbye!" called their friends and relatives. "Come back soon and tell us about the great king."

With a clattering of hooves and a billow of dust, the travellers set out on their journey.

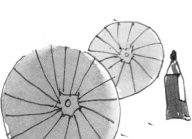

They travelled for many weeks through countryside just like their own. There were plenty of inns to stay at, with good food and friendly people.

Weeks went by, and months, and soon there were fewer towns and smaller villages. The country became hot and dry, and the yellow sand stretched as far as the eye could see.

Yet each night, when the skies were clear, Lao Zhou and Jiang unpacked their instruments and studied the stars.

And always the "royal star" sparkled and beckoned them towards the west.

One night, as the astronomers sat talking quietly together, Little Han heard a noise. It came from the direction of the road, but it sounded like thunder.

S uddenly, powerful horses seemed to come from every direction at once as robbers rode into the camp. Little Han saw the moonlight flashing on their drawn swords.

"Hand over your treasure or you die," shouted the leader.

Lao Zhou stumbled to his feet and began pulling boxes and caskets from the carriage. Jiang brought rolls of silk from the tents and held them out to the greedy hands.

Lao Meng crouched silently on the ground, watching. Little Han stood frozen, unable to move or cry out.

inally the men turned their horses and sped back along the road, their rough laughter melting away into the night.

Lao Meng was the first to speak. "Do not be afraid," she smiled. "We have our lives. And we have not lost everything." She moved aside to reveal the precious sight tube and star charts, safely hidden under her robe.

Little Han ran to the broken carriage. The plain wooden box was still there. He let out a joyful shout. "The presents for the king. The robbers didn't even notice them!"

Gently he opened the lid and moved aside a corner of cloth wrapping. Something inside gleamed a pale golden colour. His own gift was safe!

"We cannot go on now," sighed Lao Zhou. "It is too dangerous."

"But then we shall never learn the secret of the 'royal star'!" cried Little Han.

"If we are to know, we shall need help, Little Han," said Lao Meng gently.

"Let us sleep and in the morning we will decide," said Jiang.

The travellers woke suddenly the next morning. Someone was calling to them.

Little Han ran out of the tent, his heart beating wildly. But it was not the robbers. A tall stranger stood at the head of a long camel train.

The man's name was Sekundar. He was a merchant from a land far away to the west. He, too, was travelling from China, with his pack camels laden with silks.

Lao Zhou explained why they were travelling and told the merchant about the robbers.

Sekundar laughed. "This road is a dangerous one to travel alone. But you may come along with me. I know this road well and my men can protect you."

Lao Meng smiled at Little Han. "Here is the help we need," she said.

For long months they travelled, wondering at the people and places they passed. Each day, as they rode, Sekundar taught them to speak Greek, the language of all the western lands. Each night Lao Zhou and Jiang plotted their course by the night sky. And always the "royal star" went on before them, brighter than ever.

One day, they came to a place where the road divided into two great highways.

"My friends," said Sekundar, "this is the place where I must leave you. Continue along the western road until you come to the city near the great sea. There, also, wise men study the stars. They will help you find your king."

The sun was setting as the weary travellers climbed the final hill and saw the great city.

The sky glowed pink. The ancient walls and turrets seemed to be made of pure gold. High above, where the sky was darkening into a velvet blue, the "royal star" shone down.

Little Han breathed a long sigh. "This must be the place," he said. "Surely the king lives here."

The travellers approached the city gates.

"Open up," called Jiang. "We come from the land of China. We are looking for the great king who has been born in your city."

As the guards hurried to open the gates, Lao Meng spoke quietly, "Lao Zhou, I sense great danger in this place. Say as little as you can and be very careful."

The astronomers were taken straight to the royal palace. The king did not rise from his throne, or greet the visitors. He gave them no tea or rice cakes.

"What's this I hear?" he roared. "A new king? Born here in my country?"

"So the stars seem to say, my Lord," replied Lao Zhou, "but we may be mistaken."

The king called for his advisers. They hastily consulted their scrolls and whispered to the king. Then the great ruler seemed to change his mind. He smiled and called the travellers to come closer.

"It seems," he beamed, "that a future king may have been born in a town to the south. So please go and find him, and then come and tell me all about it. I shall be delighted to go and greet him myself." His smile was wide but his eyes held an evil glitter. Little Han did not like this king at all.

Hastily the travellers left the great city and turned towards the south. Even by day it seemed that the "royal star" glowed and sparkled, beckoning them on.

Later that day, as they approached a village, small and plain like any other, the stars seemed to dip low in the sky.

"Look, the stars!" cried Little Han excitedly.

"This must be the place," breathed Lao Meng.

"But there is no palace," said Little Han.

As they watched, a woman came out of a tiny house. She held the hand of a small boy.

The visitors fell silent as the "royal star" slowly faded and disappeared into the evening sky.

"Who is this, that has power to change the course of the stars?" whispered Lao Zhou, covering his face.

"The power that moves the stars is the same power that gives life to a child," cried Lao Meng. "We have found the king we seek."

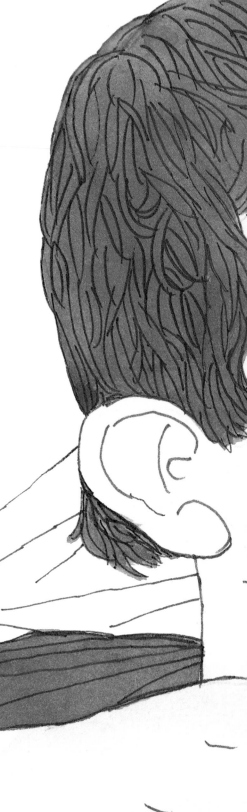

Inside the house they opened the wooden box.

"Lady, we bring you gifts," said Lao Zhou. "Sweet-smelling frankincense, whose smoke is a reminder of the link between the heavens and the earth."

"And myrrh," said Lao Meng, stepping forward. "Precious, yet bitter. A sign of the suffering a king must bear to look after his people. For we have no doubt that your son will be a king."

"I bring you a robe," said Jiang, "woven without a seam. Its colour is the plainest brown, but it is fashioned from pure silk."

Finally, Little Han took from the box his most precious possession. He unwrapped it and held it in his hand for a long moment.

He thought of his grandfather who had given it to him when his mother and father died. And of the generations of his family, stretching back into time, who had kept this treasure safe.

Then he held it out to the boy. It was a lion, made of the purest gold.

The child took the lion, laughing with delight and turning it in his small hands.

"It is for you," said Little Han. "Gold, for a king."

The perfume of frankincense and myrrh filled the room. The golden lion glowed in the lamplight and the little boy reached out and took Little Han by the hand.

Peace and happiness welled up inside his heart and Little Han knew that he would never be truly lonely again.

The travellers did not return to tell cruel King Herod about the baby. Another story says they went home by a different route.

We do not know what happened to them, or what adventures they met with on the long road back to the east.

But we have heard about the "royal star" and the birth of a baby boy who was to become a different kind of king.

We know him by his name — Jesus — and we call this the Christmas story. It is the greatest story in the world.